MOONDRAGON IN THE MOSQUE GARDEN

Written by El-Farouk Khaki and Troy Jackson

Illustrated by Katie Commodore

Papa T sticks his head into Tajalli's room and laughs. "I'm glad you like the clothes I made, but now put them on, please! We don't want to be late."

3

Lots of people stop to greet them with hugs and kisses, saying "As-Salaam Alaikum!" and "Eid Mubarak!"

Tajalli sees his cousins Mujtaba and Aasiya and they run toward each other. Some people can't tell them apart but Tajalli always can.

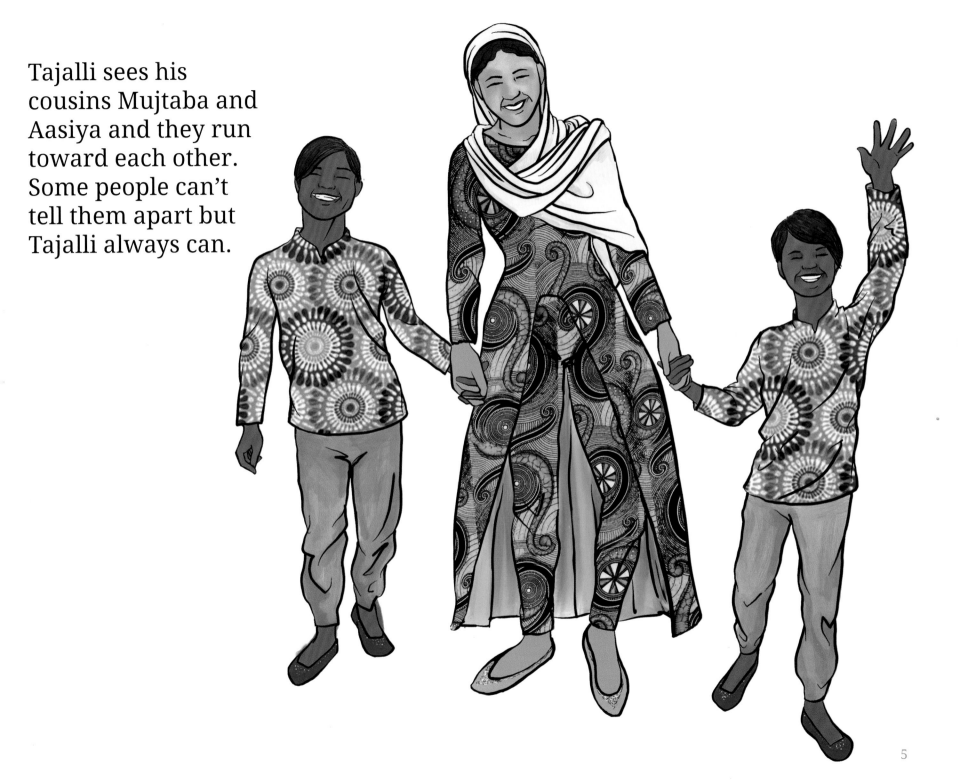

Tajalli loves how his Unity Mosque is grey on the outside but full of colour on the inside. On a sunny day every room is full of bright rainbows, and the biggest ones go where the leader of prayers stands – and today that's his big cousin Hajjar! Her first time!

Tajalli, Mujtaba and Aasiya cover Hajjar in hugs and kisses before she goes to prepare.

7

Aasiya points to the old garden and says quietly, "Later, let's go outside." Tajalli looks out and just for a minute, it seems like he sees something. Something purple? "Yes!" he says, just as Daddy E calls them all in to stand for prayers.

After the prayers – which Hajjar does perfectly! – Auntie Amina starts to talk about the earth and stewardship. Tajalli and his cousins bounce and fidget and try to follow. Auntie Amina gives them a stern look and says "We must ALL keep the promise to take care of our Mother Earth."

After the talk finishes, Tajalli and his cousins run for the sweets table and collect as many as they can. Eid al-Fitr is full of sweets and presents!

Tajalli, Mujtaba, and Aasiya meet under the table with the lime green table cloth, so they can sneak out before their parents notice. Just when they get giggly and wiggly, Tajalli's Papa T sticks his head under the table with a smile and says, "Aha!" The three cousins run outside, laughing.

When they get outside into the sunshine, the twins snap off some twigs and whack wildly at the tall grass as they run off.

Tajalli kicks an empty bottle for a while. Aasiya pulls flowers off a big bush and fills the fountain with them while Mujtaba eats caramels and holds each wrapper up to wiggle until the wind carries it off.

Suddenly, the wrappers start to fly back toward them, and empty bottles, and other litter too! It's SO gross.

"Who is doing that? Stop it please!" Tajalli shouts.
"Come on guys, let's get out of here," calls out Mujtaba.

Out of nowhere, a voice like a bubbling stream says: "Didn't you learn ANYTHING from your Auntie Amina's sermon?" The kids look all over until they see a shimmering, hazy, purple shape of a small...dragon?

A breeze blows through the garden, ruffling its silvery feathers. "You couldn't pronounce my name," says the dragon, tossing its head, "so just call me Moondragon. That's what I am."

Tajalli asks: "Where did you come from? How come you can talk?"

"What's a Moondragon?" asks Mujtaba.

Moondragon just smiles and shrugs.

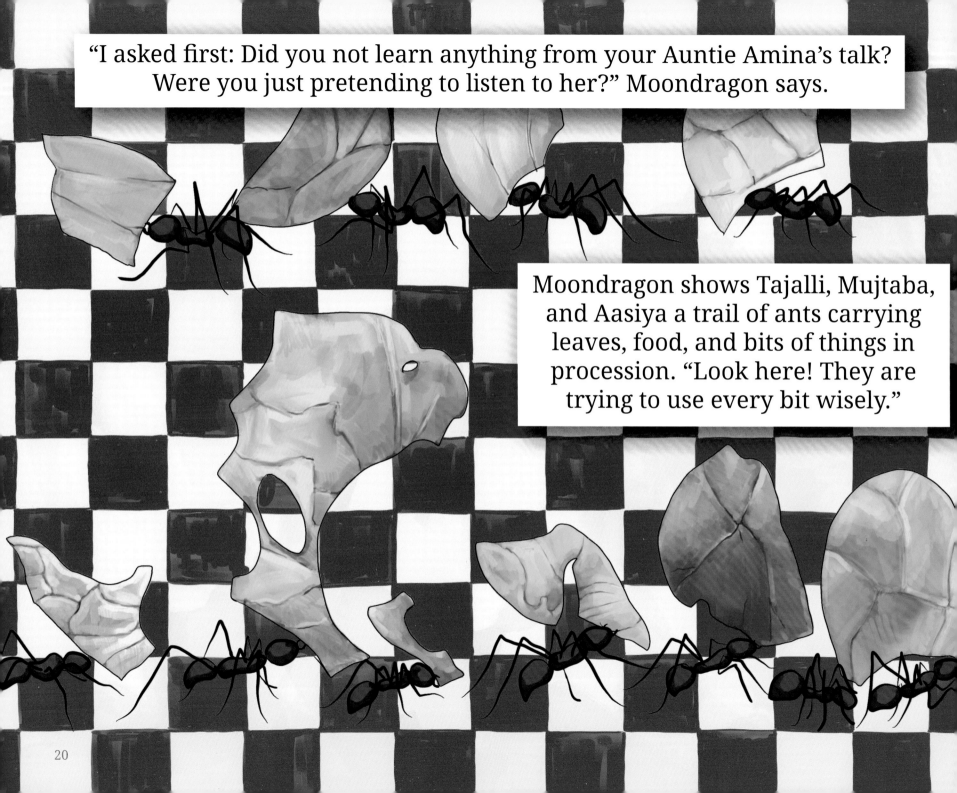

"I asked first: Did you not learn anything from your Auntie Amina's talk? Were you just pretending to listen to her?" Moondragon says.

Moondragon shows Tajalli, Mujtaba, and Aasiya a trail of ants carrying leaves, food, and bits of things in procession. "Look here! They are trying to use every bit wisely."

Then it waves them on to a bunch of overgrown water lilies and points at them. They're full of bees! "Here are more small things, doing their jobs so we get plenty of flowers and vegetables. So cute!" says Moondragon, petting their fuzzy bums gently.

In a blink of the Moondragon's silvery eyelashes, all three kids are shrunk down to the size of bees.

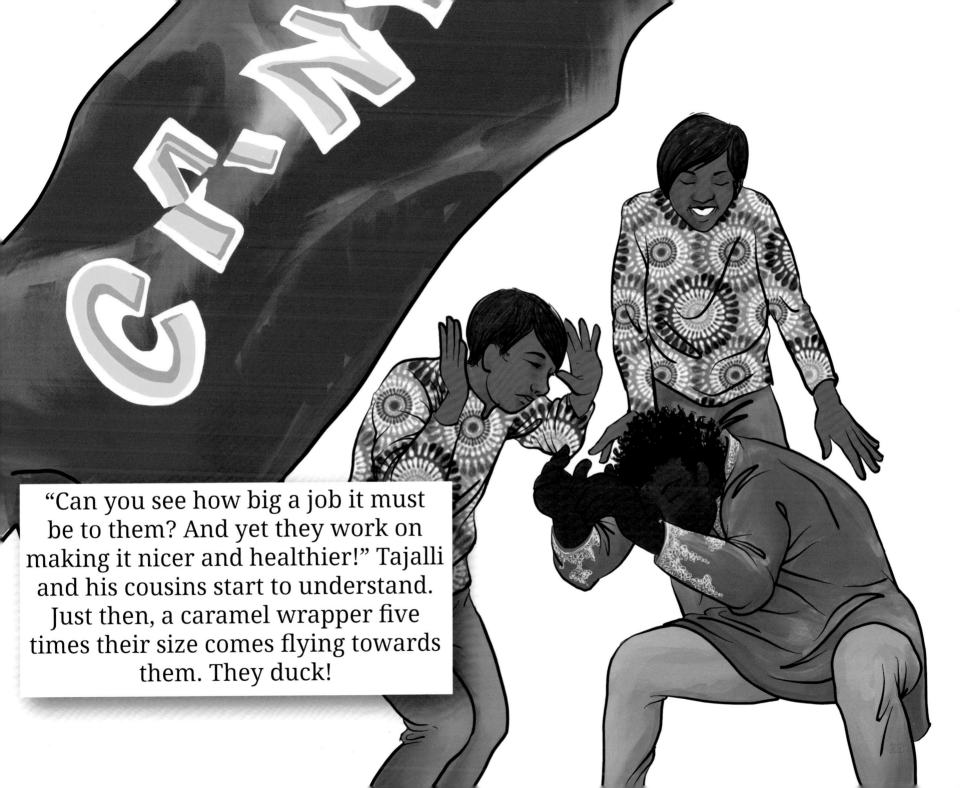

"Can you see how big a job it must be to them? And yet they work on making it nicer and healthier!" Tajalli and his cousins start to understand. Just then, a caramel wrapper five times their size comes flying towards them. They duck!

Moondragon makes everyone their regular size again with a flick of its tail. "It's a lot of work to care for the earth, and you three have been very disrespectful to this garden. So now you cannot leave until it's all cleaned. If you don't help, you will be trapped in this garden forever!"

Then Moondragon starts to laugh. "Just kidding!"

"No one can make you give the earth your love and care. But I hope you will choose to join me and the ants and the bees." The kids all nodded and smiled. "We will!"

Tajalli and the twins help Moondragon. They pick up the garbage, trim the plants, scrub the stones, clear the fountain, and water everything. In no time, the garden is looking beautiful...but their Eid outfits are not.

Daddy E and Papa T and Grandma Rose come outside, looking for Tajalli and his cousins. Just before they're going to scold the children, they notice how beautiful the garden looks.

Tajalli says: "Our friend Moondragon made us the size of bees and encouraged us to be nice to mother earth!"

"So imaginative, these children," Grandma Rose says. "Looks like Auntie Amina really inspired you! Now, let's get home and clean so we can go visit friends!"